RINGO DINGO
FINDS A NEW HOME

by:
JEAN EDWARDS

To order additional copies of this book, contact:
Xlibris
844-714-8691
www.Xlibris.com
Orders@Xlibris.com

ISBN: Softcover   978-1-6641-9570-7
         Hardcover   978-1-6641-9569-1
         EBook   978-1-6641-9568-4

Print information available on the last page

Rev. date: 11/02/2021

Ringo Dingo
Finds a New Home

Ringo Dingo was born in the outback of Eastern Australia. His first six months were happy, hunting for food by day and cuddling next to his mother in their den at night. As time passed by, his mother began teaching him all he should know to live on his own.

One day Ringo wandered from the den to the edge of the great grassy plain. Wandering on, he soon lost his bearings and became lost. He could not find his mother or his den. Ringo sat down and thought about his predicament until he fell asleep. Awaking from his nap, he made a decision. If he couldn't find his old home, he would search for a new one.

Hearing a thump, thump, thump sound behind him he turned...and what did he see but a small tan animal hopping along on his hind legs. He looked like a kangaroo, he hopped like a kangaroo, but he was much smaller than a kangaroo.

"Hello," the animal said. "My name is Polly, and I am a wallaby. What is your name my furry stranger?"

"I am Ringo Dingo. I am a wild dog, but I am friendly. I have decided to look for a home of my own. Would you like to come with me?"

Polly thought for a moment. She had always thought that some day she would find a special friend, but she thought it would be another wallaby. Finally, Polly said, "All right, I will go with you. I have no family and I, too, need to find my own home."

Soon they reached a place on the grassy plain where eucalyptus trees were standing here and there.

"This is a nice place for a home", Ringo Dingo declared. Suddenly they heard a roar and they looked back and saw that fire was burning the tall grasses and trees.

"We must run away," Polly cried.

"Yes," Ringo agreed. "But wait. I see something in that eucalyptus tree."

Taking a closer look they discovered a small gray roly-poly bundle with large eyes clinging in fear to one of the upper eucalyptus branches.

"Quick Polly," said Ringo. "We must find a mango or kiwi branch on the ground that we can put against that tree. We must save that frightened little fellow!"

The two ran through the grass until they found a branch that had fallen from a tree in a storm.

It was not long enough to reach the small animal, so Ringo said, "Quick, Polly, get on my back and hold the branch up against the tree!"

It was not easy as the branch swayed in Polly's small hands, but finally it rested against the eucalyptus tree and the little animal climbed down.

"Thank you so much! My name is Viola Koala", and I am a marsupial", she declared. "We must hurry before the fire gets closer!"

Viola rode on Ringo's back and they were soon over the hill.

The three walked steadily away from the direction of the fire.

Ringo looked at Polly and said, "Polly, here are some mangoes and kiwi fruit – put them in your pouch so you will have something to eat later. I will gather some eucalyptus leaves for Viola!"

Polly said, "What about you Ringo? You will be hungry also!"

"Don't worry about me," he replied. " I can dig up some tasty grubs anywhere!"

Suddenly the soft sandy ground gave way beneath them. Down, down, down they went. As they fell they all thought it was the end of them. When they finally reached the bottom with a "Ka-plop," they sat up and looked around. They had landed on a pile of soft moss.

Ringo declared, "This is a den of some kind. I hope it belongs to a friendly animal. I will protect you no matter what!"

Polly put her arms around Viola, who was accustomed to living in trees, and did not feel safe.

They were comforting each other when they heard a sound. Out from a hole in the wall of the pit came a strange looking animal.

"Hello," he said in a friendly manner. "I am Wilbur Wombat and I don't have company very often. You may call me "Willie". You are welcome here."

Polly reached into her pouch and brought forth a ripe red mango. Offering it to willie she explained, "We fell into your home by accident. Please accept this fruit from us."

"Thank you", Willie answered politely.

"I am glad to have you visit, but how did you plan to return to the upper earth?"

"We have no way of returning. How do you reach the upper earth?", Polly asked.

Willie laughed. "Have no fear, Willie is here! I leave my home here below often to forage for plants and other food. I will take you back, but you must not tell anyone of my tunnels. Just follow me."

Willie Wombat led them through a labyrinth of tunnels until they finally emerged from the tunnel entrance that was hidden beneath a growth of thick bushes.

Lo and behold, they found themselves on the bank of the river. Willie bid them good-bye and disappeared back into the tunnel.

"The river will stop the fire, it cannot cross the water," Ringo said.

Polly spoke up, "But how can we get across to safety? I can't swim and neither can Viola!"

Suddenly a large scaly head came out of the water. It was a huge crocodile. "Get on my back," the crocodile offered.

"No," Viola cried. "You will eat us all!"

"Don't worry", the crocodile said. "I am a friendly crocodile. My friends call me "Brock the Croc." I will not harm you. I have a full stomach because I have just eaten turtle eggs, and besides, you are all too furry. I don't like fur in my teeth. I give you my word that I will deliver you all safely to the other side of the river.

With the fire creeping steadily towards them, the three climbed on the back of the crocodile. True to his words, the crocodile carried them across the river to safety.

When they reached the bank across the river they thanked the crocodile and examined their surroundings.

The riverbank was steep but they struggled and made it up to the top where they came upon a strange animal they had never seen before.

"I say," Ringo called out. "We are looking for a place to make our new home. Can you help us?"

The animal hesitated a moment, then he replied, "Hello there, old boy," he said to Ringo. "My name is Percival Platypus. I live in this muddy bank and I have many tunnels through the mud. You are welcome to make your home in one of my tunnels."

The three looked at each other in astonishment. This furry animal with a snout like a duck's bill seemed very friendly indeed!

Ringo thought the situation over, then slowly shook his head. "We would be most happy with a home in a mango or kiwi grove. We truly appreciate your kind offer and we would enjoy visiting, but we would prefer living further from the river."

"I understand," Percival replied. "You will always be welcome here. I wish you good luck on your quest! Now I must return to my den. My mate and I must keep our 3 eggs warm, for soon they will hatch and we will hear the patter of little webbed feet. I would go with you, but my home is here."

The three watched as the platypus waddled on his webbed feet towards the river and his many tunneled home.

Onward they traveled until they came upon a huge orchard of eucalyptus and fruit trees, but wait!

They could not gather any of the fruit because a tall fence had been put around the trees as far as they could see.

"This would be a great place for our new home," Ringo declared.

"Yes," said Polly. "It would have been perfect!"

They followed the fence until they came to a gate with a sign attached that read "Wildlife Refuge".

The friends waited at the gate, and soon an attendant in a green and khaki uniform discovered them.

"Well! What have we here?" the attendant exclaimed. "I guess you three are looking for a home. Welcome to our Wildlife Refuge!", he said, as he opened the gate and let them in.

Ringo and his friends had
found their new home!